NORBERT

For
Leon
xxx

A TEMPLAR BOOK

First published in the UK in 2018 by Templar Publishing,
an imprint of Kings Road Publishing, part of the Bonnier Publishing Group,
The Plaza, 535 King's Road, London, SW10 0SZ
www.templarco.co.uk
www.bonnierpublishing.com

1 3 5 7 9 10 8 6 4 2

ISBN 978-1-78741-220-0

This book was typeset in MrsEaves
The illustrations were created digitally
Edited by Katie Haworth
Designed by Olivia Cook

Printed in China

NORBERT

Joanna Boyle

templar
books

There was once a penguin called Norbert who lived in Antarctica.
It was a big, cold and lonely place, but Norbert wasn't lonely at all.

He had heaps of family and friends!
There was only one problem . . .

They didn't have much in common.

One day something unexpected washed up onshore.
It was a flyer for a musical in the big city!

Norbert rushed to show everyone.

But they just weren't interested.

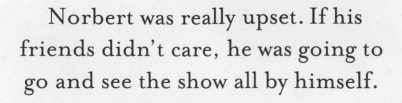

Norbert was really upset. If his friends didn't care, he was going to go and see the show all by himself.

He got in his boat and sailed away.
It was not a fun journey.

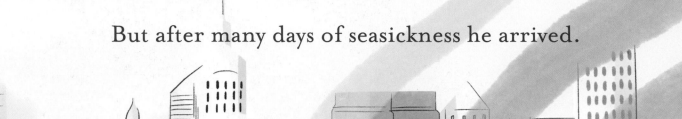

But after many days of seasickness he arrived.

The city was huge!

Statue

Norbert wandered through the streets taking in the sights.

SOPHIE'S SOFAS

Sweenie's BARBERS

buttercup Cafe

OPEN

Post box

Cats

He thought about writing a letter home but then, just around the corner, he saw . . .

. . . the THEATRE!

THE SOUND OF MEERKATS

Theatre
GEESE
THE
MUSICAL!
THE SOUND OF
MEERKATS

GEESE

Shops

Books Books Books

Books

Inside, there was a hum of excitement as
the orchestra tuned their instruments.

Then the show began!

Norbert was transfixed!

He laughed . . .

cried . . .

booed . . .

gasped . . .

shivered . . .

and by the end . . .

Outside, he joined a long line to audition.

All sorts of people stood up and sang.

It was pretty impressive.

But finally Norbert got his turn.

He thought it went quite well . . .

. . . but he didn't exactly get what he was hoping for.

Norbert got all sorts of jobs around the theatre. Some were glamorous . . .

laa!

BANG!

. . . and some were not so glamorous.

EEp!

He thought about writing home, but he couldn't think what to say.

And then, one day, Norbert got his big break.

Norbert stood up on stage,
summoned all his courage
and sang . . .

The crowd went wild!

They whooped, whistled, clapped and threw
bouquet after bouquet of flowers.

Norbert was a star.

The life of a star is very busy.

Norbert went to parties, sat in limousines
and sang in every musical on Broadway.

He thought about writing home,
but the moment never seemed quite right.

Soon, Norbert won a big shiny award.

He stood up to make his speech,
but something felt wrong . . .

He ran outside, and back to his fancy hotel.

Then, FINALLY, Norbert wrote a letter home.

He tried to put lots of things in it, like how sorry he was
he'd gone off in a huff and how much he missed them all.

It took him all night to write. The next morning he posted it.

He hoped it would arrive okay.

A few weeks later the phone rang.

Norbert ran to the harbour and got on the first boat headed south.

The wind screeched and the waves rocked but Norbert didn't care.

And finally . . .

. . . he made it home, where there was something special waiting for him.

It was the best surprise
Norbert had ever had.

THE
END.

More picture books from Templar:

ISBN: 978-1-78370-631-0

ISBN: 978-1-78741-054-1

ISBN: 978-1-78741-234-7

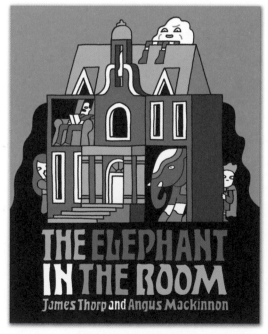

ISBN: 978-1-78370-773-7